# Crossfaded in Narnia

Ian Kappos

**Crossfaded in Narnia**
by Ian Kappos
ISBN: 978-1-908125-65-1

Cover Art by David Rix

Publication Date: July 2018



Earlier versions of these stories appeared in: *Bartleby Snopes* ("My Childhood as a Student of Chemical Warfare," May 2013); *FLAPPERHOUSE #5* ("The Key of Joy," under the title "Undergrowth," March 2015); *Pravic #3* ("Scoring for Ridnour Before High Tide," June 2013); *Deimos eZine #2.1* ("Hervé," March 2013); *The Breakroom Stories* ("Tell Me More," January 2016)

*Dedicated to the memory of Evan Kincade*

*November 26th, 1990 – November 9th, 2016*

# Acknowledgements

First of all, endless thanks to David Rix. To have my debut chapbook released by Eibonvale Press—a publisher of so many great titles and some of my favorite writers—is nothing short of a dream for me. Without David's passion, keen eye, and belief in these stories, this little book wouldn't be possible.

Thanks also to the editors who originally published these stories: Gwendolyn Edward, Carl Fuerst, David Gill, Jacen Kemp, Joe O'Brien, Nathaniel Tower.

For their guidance, support, and encouragement: Steve Cirrone, Brendan Connell, Ricardo Cortez Cruz, Joshua Edwards, Brian Evenson, Josh Fernandez, Janice Lee, Scott Nicolay, Doug Rice, Mary Rickert, John Shirley.

My write-or-dies: Kate Foster, Jack Hill, Derek Tollefson.

Friends who helped me with these stories in their many versions: Natalie Armstrong, Ian Boalt, Amy Bush, Amy da Silva, Zacc Dukowitz, Mila Jaroniec, Elias Kuhlmann, Corley Miller, Andrew Palumbo, Maria Pogosyan, Rob Rice, Zach Roth, Hannah Rubin.

Additional thanks: Krista Bautista, Genelle Chaconas, Joe Donohoe, Jackson Griffith, Craig Hancock, Tyler King, Mitch Steiger, Jordan Traller, Joanna C. Valente, Larry Vossler, Luke Wortley.

My family: Carol & John Kappos, Corby Lawton, Aline O'Brien, Becky & Dan Petrie, June Petrie, Allison & Brian Spreadborough.

# Contents

# My Childhood as a Student of Chemical Warfare

After my mom got a job, she started coming home late at night. She'd tread down the hallway, skin squeaking, the smell of lavender trailing in her wake. In the morning I'd walk down that hallway on my way to the bathroom, stepping over dampened floorboards, and, under the bathroom light, find a syrupy purple film drying into the bottoms of my feet. Often I had to double-shower. Since my mom had been job-hunting for a while, I didn't mind putting up with this, content to continue doing so if it meant she was happy.

But then she brought Danny, her new boyfriend, home.

My birthday came. With our slightly increased financial security, my mom decided to splurge, getting me a big cake. She presented it to me in the dining room, where it brightened and dimmed under the naked, flickering bulb above the table. The cake was shaped like a bee pollinating a flower. It was quite ornate.

"Say thank you to your mother," said Danny through his gasmask.

"Thank you, Mom."

Because Danny had a strict policy of No Smoke at Home, my mom left the candles unlit. I pretended to blow them out while my new dad looked on intensely.

Danny, despite his qualms about smoke, didn't seem to mind the smell of the house, or the damp spots. Also, my mom said, he didn't drink. She didn't have a sense of smell, so she had to take him at his word.

School was rough. All my clothes were white. No matter how much bleach I used, there was always a splotch of purple here, a ghost of violet there. The other kids teased me for it. I'd explain to them that my mom worked in a factory, she worked with machines. And they'd say, oh, they bet she did.

At home, though we had never had the money to afford a wide selection of food, somehow—as our meals began to rotate according to Danny's wildly shifting moods—our options still managed to dwindle. On those nights when Danny was happy, we ate cauliflower steeped in butter.

"Sweetie," my mom said to me on one of Danny's happy nights, "eat your cauliflower." Since taking the job at the factory, her skin had grown as smooth as a doll's. And—I speculated,

10

recalling that day's biology class—probably as biodegradable, too. Which is to say, not very biodegradable at all.

"Yeah," Danny said, "eat your fucking cauliflower."

My mom didn't mind Danny's swearing. In fact, she found it endearing.

"It's high in fiber, son," Danny went on. "You need your fucking fiber."

He had gotten into the habit of calling me *son*.

"Yes, dear," my mom chimed in. "Listen to Danny. He knows a lot about fiber."

Apparently that wasn't all Danny knew a lot about. He was also a self-proclaimed expert on World War I, or as he called it, "the Great War, fuck the rest." Sometimes, in his better moods, he'd talk about trenches, about the birth of biological warfare. (Here he'd start to breathe heavily, seemingly in the grips of a great lust, through the bulky apparatus on his face.) When after talking for a while he noticed my eyes going glassy, he'd cuff me behind the ear and say, "You're blind! You've been hit!"

And that's how things went.

Soon Danny started taking me to school in his truck. He was never late. "Late," according to Danny, "is either dead or pregnant."

I had to start cutting things from my routine in order to fit his schedule. The first thing to go was my morning shower. My first day without it, a deep purple seeped through my socks, and when I took them off my feet were absurdly swollen, as though someone had crushed them with a hammer.

It should come as no surprise that my days at school went along much as they had before, if not worse. Day by day, the prospect of a normal social life grew more and more unlikely.

Then one day, I came home to find my mom back from work early, packing things into boxes. I asked what was going on.

She said, "We're moving into Danny's parents' house. They're rich, you know."

Her face elasticized into a grin.

Around that time, a lilac fungus had started to grow between my toes. My sleep began to suffer, my appetite diminished. My skin paled, bags swelled underneath my eyes. Other kids started to keep their distance, as if fearing they'd contract something.

I was open to change.

The next morning Danny dropped me off at the bus stop. "I gotta take care of some shit," he told me, his gasmask muffling the consonants of his words into radio grit. I started to step out of the truck, but he grabbed me by the shoulder and pulled me back. The gasmask crept in so close that I could see my fuzzy reflection in it—and behind my reflection, the violet of his eyes. The smell of booze clawed up my nostrils. I blinked back tears.

"Don't listen to any of those Armenians in your class," the gasmask said. "They're all liars and deserved whatever it is they're lying to you about."

"Okay," I said, choking. I hopped out of the truck.

To pass the time I walked in circles around the bus stop, trying to crush the itchiness in my feet. I examined my fleshy, bruise-colored wrist. I had this thing I liked to do sometimes, I guess you could call it a coping mechanism. What I did was, when I got anxious, I liked to pretend I owned a watch. I would raise my forearm and look at the spot where my imaginary watch was, and I'd count back the seconds in anticipation of the imaginary appointment I had, the place where I had to be in fifteen, fourteen, thirteen, twelve seconds from now. There, walking around in circles at the bus stop, it occurred to me that Danny's parents might, after my mom and I moved into their house, buy me a watch. They were, after all, *rich*. If I had a watch, I'd always know what time it was. If I always knew what time it was, I'd always know where I had to be. If I started paying more attention to Time, maybe Time might start paying more attention to me.

Besides, all the other boys in my class had already started growing armpit hair, and here I was still dealing with this foot fungus.

# The Key of Joy

It took me until the river to realize what it was. It took months of being in a daze, of half-hearted meetings with school counsellors. It took puzzled sneers from classmates and quiet rejections on the basketball court, it took questions that my foster parents ignored, and yearnings for human touch. It took slinking down residential streets and slipping from one front-yard shadow to the next, crowning the levee, and crossing the railroad tracks—it took my nostrils burning in the cold—to realize what it was that I felt. Homesickness. I felt homesick, but for which home, I didn't know.

Our feet sprayed gravel from the tracks down into the darkness as we began the descent toward the river. Seamus pointed to an outlet in the murk. I drew closer, looked. The tree wasn't like the other trees but just how I couldn't say. All I could see from where we stood was that it craned over the water, and had something on it. "It's old," Seamus said. "I looked it up online."

The year was 1999, the last year that it would be cool for fourteen-year-old boys to listen to boy bands. Though neither of us was cool, we were as much victims of circumstance as anybody our age.

Seamus maintained the lead, pulling us deeper into the underbrush. The moon lazed close; beyond the tangle of branches, the river shone wrinkles of silver. Frogs croaked, mosquitoes buzzed, there were tracers from dragonflies. Through it all, Seamus spearheaded our campaign, still blissfully unaware of or unwilling to address my nerves. It was summer and we both wore denim shorts and polo shirts.

"Just around this bend," he said.

I tripped over a rock, my foot slurping into the gummy earth alongside the river. The water played at my shoes. Tugging my foot loose, I looked up and saw then what made the tree different, the thing hugging like a sleeve around a branch, bright and pulsating between colors, drab earthy green sharpening into eye-stinging neon.

Seamus was stopped in front of it, and I was still lagging far enough behind that all it took was the river's watery moan to swallow up what he said. I asked him to repeat himself, but either he didn't hear or he chose not to answer. The roots of the tree were half in the ground, half in the river. On the surface of the sleeve, there were little wormy things, fawning from it and dancing languidly in different directions, like tentacles.

I came up alongside Seamus, panting.

"Maybe a lichen?" he said.

I peered closer.

"I wish I'd brought my camera," he continued, then cursed.

The branch wilted toward the river, leafless, defeated. Seamus wagged his head as if trying to shake a spider's web from it then took another squelching step forward, extending his arm.

This time of year, trees weren't supposed to be dying, I'd learned at least that much from excursions through the park with my mom when we had to hide out from my dad. Growing up in the city, trees were rare and foreign things to me, and I'd found them alluring. Sometimes during the fights back at the apartment, I'd return to the park on my own to spend more time with the trees. I never learned their names or their species, but I liked it that way. To me they felt more like relics, like lost artifacts, when they didn't have names.

The tentacles turned toward Seamus, and he hopped back, alarmed. They were like thick emerald hairs that had been rubbed by a balloon.

One day in my room back in the city—after my dad had left 'for good'—I was inspecting a deteriorating wall when I uncovered a litter of rats. I fed them pieces from a brick of cheese—the only thing left in the fridge—mostly the moldy parts but some good parts, too, and kept the rest for myself. The way they all looked up at me with cloudy eyes was kind of like these tentacles: blind, but discerning.

"Let's go back up to the tracks," Seamus said. There was an urgency in his voice and he was short of breath. Though I wanted to stand there a little longer looking at the tree, we were staying the night at his mom's house and he got to call the shots. This was the unspoken rule and I was in no place to argue.

At the top of the levee, Seamus lit a joint. It was the first time I'd seen weed, though I had smelled it before in one of my foster homes. He passed it to me and I drew on it hesitantly, coughed. I peered at him through my blurred vision and saw him nodding at me sagely, his head fusing with the moon.

Sitting on the tracks, we started talking. Or rather, Seamus started talking. This time it was about a guy named Aleister Crowley. I'd only moved to town a few months before, but it hadn't taken long to learn that I rarely knew about the things he knew about.

I was fat, had a bowl-cut and glasses. Seamus was in better shape, but his eyes were very far apart from each other, and he wore capris every day. Though I'd never seen evidence of girls liking him, he'd claimed to have gotten laid when he was ten. On this, I gave him the benefit of the doubt because I wanted to trust him. Girls didn't like me much, and this was a constant source of dejection for me.

"I'm going to loan you one of his books," Seamus was saying. "It's called *The Book of the Law*. You'll like it."

Nodding, I marvelled at the green around us, the cloudlessness, my eyes drifting across the tapestry of stars, my ears listening for, and for a second picking up on, the heartbeat of the universe. I thought of lichen. I thought of my parents. I wondered how much I resembled one of them right then, high for my very first time, face sagging. Tonight, with everything colored so differently that it was almost new again, I think I finally fully understood how small I was.

Seamus' mother took me home the next day. The Aleister Crowley book was tucked away in my backpack because Seamus was adamant that she should not see it. "Nor anyone else, for that matter," he said.

Climbing into the top bunk in the room I shared with another foster boy, I waited till I felt the coast was clear before cracking the book open. Though I tried my best to decipher it, the language was beyond my level of comprehension. I called Seamus, embarrassed. "All you really need to know," he said, "is this: love is the law, love under will." Even though it was probably my imagination, I could swear he was smirking as he said it.

I swallowed the knot in my throat. "Okay," I said.

A year later I discovered cocaine and OxyContin in the same night. Seamus and I sat in his mother's kitchen at the dinner table, naked, with a heap of off-white powder between us. He squished mounds, diced chunks of pills into chalk, mixed the two together into granulated hills, demonstrated to me with all the zeal of teenage obsession the first-rate education about the world of drugs he'd gotten from the internet. We talked at each other through the night, our mouths, dry as bark, moving too fast for our thoughts. Eventually I threw up, broke out in itches, and not long afterwards he did the same. Stubbornly unrelenting in the new confusion of our bodies, we continued to talk past each other. At one point the light flickered—not on or off, but to a brilliant emerald green, and I couldn't be sure if it was a hallucination. But then, just as quickly, it went back to normal. For a moment our feverish dialogue was blown off course.

Looking at Seamus, I noted the unease in his eyes that confirmed he'd seen it, too. He made a weird joke about lens filters, which I nervously laughed at.

While Seamus tended to compare things with the mechanics of light, the parameters of composition, I could tell that with the flickering light a new dimension had been added to his understanding, creating a sort of paranoia, as if he half-expected the bulb to go green again and plunge us into the fabric of the earth.

His mother wasn't home. We were fifteen and about to start attending separate high schools. I'd moved into a new foster home. Two years into my teens, and I was already bitterly accustomed to abandonment.

Later that night, Seamus started talking differently.

"Next year…" He started scratching his collarbone. I waited for him to go on, but he seemed to have lost track of his thoughts. I found myself, against my will, studying the hard line of his clavicle, the toxic sweat beading there, wondering what it must taste like.

Then he coughed and kept coughing until he had to go outside to puke in the garden. When he returned, his skin was tightened around his eyes, his lips parted in a teeth-stained smile. "Next year," he said, "in that photography class you said you're going to take, I have something for you to think about. Think about the river at night."

I froze, feeling under my skin the crazed hammering of my pulse. This was the first time he'd said anything, since it happened, about that night by the river now a year past. I often lay awake thinking about it, trying to recreate on the insides of my eyelids that otherworldly hue of the lichen on the tree, the tree that I couldn't name.

He went on: "Your teacher's going to say whatever your teacher's going to say, maybe they'll say some good stuff, but just think about this first, think about all the things a camera *won't* let you do." He was no longer smiling, but staring at me intently, breathing heavily through his mouth. "Or, better yet—what your memory won't let you do."

I watched his finger trace a path across the table, gray-white specks collecting on the oils around the cuticles.

"There are things we weren't designed to remember," Seamus said. "That's why we study." Then he laughed.

What did he remember? I wondered. And what didn't he?

By the time I thought of something to say, he was already going on about something else. Eyes half-lidded, I leaned back in my chair and let his talking happen to me, my fingers worming through my new tuft of chest hair. I tried, mentally, to will a breeze into the room.

I didn't know it then, but this would be the last time Seamus and I saw each other. Halfway through the fall semester, he was shot and killed on his way home from school. No bullet casing near the crime scene, no leads on a murderer or a motive. The only details I knew were these: he'd been wearing capris and a white T-shirt smudged with grass stains, the titles of his textbooks had all been crossed out and replaced with Latin names of flora, and the battery compartment of his camera had been stuffed with weeds and honeysuckle.

A week or so prior to his death, he'd come out of the closet.

For just the second time in the short while I'd known him, I detected unease in his voice. I smashed the phone to my ear, wanting to experience this fully but also feeling a certain amount of guilt about it. When he said he'd understand if I didn't want to hang out with him anymore, no hard feelings, I laughed. I told him, "Don't be ridiculous," though secretly I feared that my foster mom was listening over the phone in the living room. It was a very religious family.

Paranoid and disoriented, I offered Seamus the only words that came to me, and hoped they'd be enough. I told him, "You're my only friend."

And this time it wasn't my imagination: Seamus' smile, over the phone, was a crackling of fibers, like a tree outgrowing its bark. "Love is the law," he intoned theatrically.

"Love under will," I said. Then we hung up.

Seamus had been the most alive thing I ever knew—I'd never met somebody so impassioned, never seen a person yearn for anything so much as I had seen him yearn for facts, categories, designations. The camera found inches from his lifeless hand—merely the latest in a series of his strategies to make sense of the world. To me, his coming out had seemed no more than a minor plot point in a narrative arc that in just a short span of time had taken him from the pits of the earth to the astral plane. Yet, all the same, this rare act of vulnerability was the last memory of him I had.

I wasn't allowed to go the funeral; by now my foster family had caught wind of all they needed to know. I screamed into my pillow as my foster brother played video games beside me.

In the following weeks I began to sneak out at night, just out into the garden behind the house—truly not much of a garden to begin with. It was riddled with wood chips and dog shit and stoic tufts of weeds. But beneath the constellations, constellations which were finally starting to look familiar, I started to learn my hands. I plunged them into the ugly topsoil. I allowed my fingers to develop minds of their own, letting them seek out their own pathways in this new network of minerals and hushed sounds, to find their own sustenance, to plant their own seeds.

In the early hours of the morning I'd return to my room, wedge my arms between my mattress and box spring, and scrape the mulch and shit and cellulose from my hands. Going to sleep, I imagined new life idling up from the nest beneath me, life rich with color and trust, inoculating me, nurturing me, and calling me not by name but by the bacteria in my stomach and the light in my eyes. The morning finally came when I awoke to my foster dad's red face hovering inches above mine. I opened my mouth but didn't say anything, just stared placidly into the eyes that had followed a trail of wet dirt from the backdoor to the foot of my bed.

I was outside myself during the beating, it was like something out of another age, an age after fire but before language, if that ever existed. He called me by name, by many names, but it all sounded like nonsense.

A few months later, the semester ended and I earned satisfactory grades, though I'd never so much as picked up a book or gone for any considerable length of time without looking out the window in anticipation of the coming spring.

On the first day of winter break my actual dad called me. With a scowl, my foster mom passed me the phone. I didn't put it to my ear until I was in my bedroom. Alone, I closed the door and sat on the edge of my bed. He had just gotten out of rehab, he told me, for the second time. He was clean now. He wanted me to come back home.

"Come back to the city," he said. "Mom, you, me—or just you and me—we'll make it work."

At first I thought that it was just bad reception, that the line had gone static, until I realized something corrosive was eating through the receiver. Then a breeze entered the room, fluttering the corner of a bedsheet and prickling my arm hairs. Everything around me had thickened, darkened. The static, I realized, was the sound of the river. I closed my eyes to a curtain of green, and a warmth spread over me, the kind of warmth you feel once you get used to the cold.

Tentacles played across the back of my hand, stretching and retracting.

"Dad," I said. "You're being immature."

I knew then that my seedlings would sprout. I put down the phone. I opened my eyes.

# Scoring for Ridnour Before High Tide

He was late and I was dopesick and it was February, the skies gushing around the bus stop awning. I huddled beneath it, my clothes flapping around me, and counted passengers hopping on, hopping off.

Eventually he emerged through the haze, his silhouette fuzzed red by taillights and electric beer ads. He sat down next to me, planted a cellophane-wrapped brown chunk in my hand. He removed a fold of bills from my other hand, got up, slid back into the fog, and I left, too.

The apartment building lobby was well-lit but no warmer, feeling like someone had just taken all the cold and wind from outside and bottled it up. I massaged the lump in my fist, the elevator rattling around me. It was all I could do just to hold my weight against the elevator wall whenever it bucked. By now I must have been closing in on the thirty-six-hour mark, that point when dopesickness nosedives into truly sinister territory.

I was doubtful Ridnour would empathize.

Keeping a supporting hand to the wall, I tottered toward the apartment.

The smell of sea salt hit me full-on as soon as I unlatched the lock. Even with all the windows shut, inside the breeze was constantly moving, springing restlessly off the walls. I pulled open the French doors of the bedroom, walked in, and collapsed into the chair beside the nightstand.

Through their syphon, Ridnour sputtered a question at me. I watched with annoyance as the slippery tassel of their filaments fidgeted across the mattress—a sickly pink color, like the inside of a raw nose.

"A gram," I confirmed.

Moaning something to the effect of *fix me up*, they began to toss their filaments about, like how an impatient cat would do with its tail. Glaring at them, I wasn't sure—never could be sure—if they saw me.

I unwrapped the cellophane, and with a switchblade I split the chunk in two. I retrieved a clean rig from a container, dipped the end into a glass of water, withdrew. Beside me, as I continued to prep, Ridnour hissed from deep inside their shell.

What I'd heard was that they'd been an anarchist, an eco-terrorist—ELF links possibly, something along those lines, but it all could've just been shooting gallery gossip. Rarely did Ridnour talk to me directly, even when I went out to cop for them. When they did speak, usually in passing, it was in half-riddles.

"One has occasion," they'd drawl, "to consider the ontological implications of a so-called independent life." But as Ridnour's tendency was to talk only after we both were loaded, my memories were fragmented.

The tar had melted down to a silky goop. Beside me, their shell pathetically pale, Ridnour spoke again but this time without ornamentation.

"Tide's coming in," they said.

My aching muscles stiffened. The salt, I could smell, was clotting the air.

"I know," I said, trying to keep my hands from shaking. "Just gimme a minute."

As if in response, the walls began to creak. I went as quickly as I could, dropping a cotton into the spoon, sucking the liquid up into the rig. Never enough time, ever.

"All right," I said, flicking the bubbles to the top. "Ready?"

Moist grumbling.

I sat on the edge of the bed and gripped one of the squirming filaments. "Be still," I said. This was always the hardest part—the others filaments, distressed, never stopped flapping in the air.

"Calm *down*."

"I'm trying," they said. "They don't listen."

I zeroed in on the pinned rope of flesh, but continued to struggle for a good angle.

They moaned impatiently.

The rest of the filaments, bunched together like a wet mop, thrashed about, getting more and more anxious as the water, which was already at my ankles, pooled in and rose.

I had to muscle it. When I drove in the needle and the roaring of the tide reached a fever pitch, Ridnour's scream of anger and disappointment soared over it. To the fizzing of the waves I depressed the plunger, the soft caress of water that had soaked through my shoes now level with the box spring.

But inside Ridnour's shell there were sounds of ecstasy. Maybe it hadn't been completely botched, there'd been a vein in there after all. With a soft regurgitation-like noise, a thick mucus sluiced out from the syphon beneath their shell. The liquid rolled off the edge of the bed, blossomed across the gathering waters.

"Tide's coming in." Their voice was bubbly and thick now, as if they'd just taken a long pull from a milk bottle. Their shell, nearly colorless a moment before, blushed.

I was already yanking my legs through the water over to the bedside table. "I'm just fixing myself up," I said. "Then I'm gone."

The floorboards groaned. As I fumbled the gear, a couple of filaments crept over to me, slipped over my thigh, as if trying to play coy. I batted them away. The reflections of the waves danced on the walls, ruddy now from Ridnour's glow.

"Wherever a tree falls..." Far-off sounding, the ghost of their voice, receding deeper inside the shell, chuckled.

"Shut up," I said.

Then a wave crashed over me and knocked me from the stool, sending the heroin sailing into the froth. I yelled and leapt in after it but thwacked against the bedpost, catching water in my mouth. Sputtering, I clutched desperately through the deluge, but by then it was gone. Flotsam.

Above me, Ridnour was trying to say something. Pulling myself out of the tide, I crawled onto the bed and stared down at the shell. I kicked it against the wall.

Their body made a *thunk*. I couldn't hear their voice anymore but I was sure they were still talking, so I reached over to the bedside table and ripped the lamp from it, threw it down hard onto the shell. There was a brief electric flash, and the red drained from the room. Then there was just the sound of water in the darkness.

"You owe me," I said, and back into the water I waded, breast-stroking down the hall to the door. It was hard to pry open, but once I managed the waves roared and crammed me through the gap. The surge buoyed me down the stairs, water fizzling and hissing over the steps. All of a sudden, I felt warmer. But it was probably, I figured, just the withdrawals.

I rode the waves all the way down.

# Hervé

We are in Josh's room smoking heroin off of a sheet of tinfoil. Well, Josh is smoking heroin off of a sheet of tinfoil. I'm fresh out of rehab and here to set a good example, so instead I'm clutching a beer and trying to develop a taste for it again.

"Can you check on Sandy?" Josh asks me after exhaling a thin gust of a smoke. He leans back in his chair, almost tips over but catches himself, readjusts the slice of tinfoil, preventing a tear of black liquid from dripping off the edge.

"Yeah," I sigh. I get up, reminding myself, as he changes the channel to a rerun of *Fantasy Island*, that I'm here for the family.

Josh has a lot of movie posters in his room— my personal favorite being an old James Bond one: *The Man with the Golden Gun*. In it, Roger Moore stands in the foreground, golden gun in hand, a young woman wrapped around his leg. In the background, Christopher Lee as Scaramanga stands menacingly beside his dwarf manservant played by Hervé Villechaize. Josh has always had this odd fascination with Villechaize, I don't know why. "He's always typecast," Josh once told me, "but you can see him, in almost every role, still trying to salvage something."

I don't know if Josh is aware that Hervé Villechaize killed himself. I've never had the heart to bring it up.

Down the hall, I open Sandy's door. She's sitting on the edge of her bed, a thin strand of saliva swivelling down the crease in her chin. She's masturbating to a Muppets movie. Her hand moves violently over the crotch of her sweatpants. In her other hand she clutches a naked Barbie doll, its head shaved on one side.

"Sandy," I say. "Sandy."

She looks at me, dragging the thread of drool across her collar. Her hand doesn't stop. Her shirt reads: VOTE FOR SANDY. On the TV, the Muppets are breaking into song.

"I'm good, Luke," she says.

I pull her wrist away from her groin. She winces at my touch and immediately I feel bad. I tell her, "Sandy, that's not okay," even though I don't know if it is or isn't. "You have to get changed into some clean clothes." I was never primed for this scenario. I think of what her parents would say, coming home and finding her like this when I'm supposed to be watching her. Maybe this isn't atypical for her. She's sixteen—for all I know they might be used to it, but still I'd rather not take the risk.

Her eyes drift back toward the television.

"Sandy, what did I just say?"

"You said you've changed, Luke—"

Then she starts vomiting, all in one motion, a curtain of brownish green cascading down her shirt, distorting its words into a cryptic anagram. I reach forward but, not knowing what to do, I just stand there watching as it continues, it goes and goes and she gasps and sputters through it—it's like a dam broke inside her; the puke falls across her clothes, the floor, my outstretched arm, and inside it, glinting, are shards of bright yellow, like regurgitated jewelry.

And then it just stops, a final burst then nothing. I use a mitten that I grab off the floor to wipe at her mouth. The mitten comes away gilded.

"Jesus, Sandy, what did you eat?"

She's breathing mainly through her nose, but it sounds regular. Grainy spittle leaks from the corners of her mouth. What would her parents want me to do in this situation?

Something crackles behind me. I turn around just as the television screen bursts, glass-shrapnel spraying in a wide trajectory across the room. I duck, but Sandy doesn't flinch. Fragments of TV bounce off her face.

I lie on the ground, on my stomach, my heart hammering in my throat. I can still hear the Muppets song in my head. Glass spills from my clothes as I get to my feet.

"Sandy," I say. My nose fills with the smell of the contents of her stomach and, beneath it, the scent of melting plastic. I start, "I'll be right b—"

But, already turning back to the empty cavern of the TV, Sandy pushes her waistband down to her knees and thrusts the head of the Barbie doll into her vagina.

"Okay, Luke."

She begins to moan, softly.

"Josh," I shout, running back into his room. He looks at me. One of his eyes goes lazy when he's loaded, but either it's never the same one, or I can just never remember correctly.

I'm panting. "Something's wrong with Sandy," I say.

He makes no sign that he's heard me. I yank the remote from his hand and turn off the TV.

"Huh?" He rolls his head around until I'm presumably centered in his vision. "What do you mean?"

"She's—" I don't know where to start. My vision swims, his walls becoming a big collage. Mixed up somewhere inside it is him, waiting for me to speak. I drank only three beers, but there was the methadone dose, too. "The TV just exploded," I say, cupping a hand to my eyes. "Didn't you hear it?"

"Exploded?"

"Yeah, dude! What the fuck!"

Peeking through my fingers, I see Josh's head loll to one side, then back to the other. "Just wait," he drawls. Then lolls again. Clockwise, counterclockwise.

"Wait for what? Your parents? What?"

Then his head jerks upward. His eyes widen with the look of someone who's just broken the surface of a frigid pool. He makes a sound, puts a hand to his temple.

A bright fluid weeps from his ear, gold as liquid sunflower.

"Just wait," he says.

He's blurring into the wall-collage again, all the James Bonds, all the villains, Hervé Villechaize's black eyes. Memories in it. Typecast, vindictive. Once, after getting high together, just to piss him off, I told him that I preferred *Moonraker*.

Sunspots light up the insides of my eyelids. I turn away.

Sandy is standing in the doorway, her pants sagging around her ankles. She's not wearing underwear, her pubic hair glistening, dotted with specks of glass. She plods into the room.

"Josh," she says.

Behind me, Josh is bucking in his chair, a steady flow of gold pouring from his ears, nose, and mouth. He gurgles, trying to say something. His feet frantically stomp. The slice of tinfoil has fallen from his hand, a rivulet of black tar dripping from it and mixing with the blinding, buttery puddle on the ground. A glow fills the room. Josh falls back, out of his chair, behind the bed. From there, out of view, he tosses light in all directions.

"Josh," Sandy says, and again I turn to the doorway.

"I'm not Josh, Sandy," I tell her. "I'm Luke."

She steps forward, her eyes fixed on the space behind the bed. She extends her Barbie doll toward it, holding it out levelly, as if Josh is right there, waiting for her to hand it over.

"Josh," she says again, and takes another step forward. The slick body of the doll catches the light.

# Tell Me More

We pulled away from the gloom of the city and, after a time, into his driveway. His lawn was a well-manicured square of green. An image popped into my head—of him plucking weeds from it, trimming an immaculate perforation between grass and concrete. He'd always seemed like the type who took his work home with him.

Since picking me up from the bus station, Doc had been mostly silent. I figured he was still trying to formulate a politically correct way to address my obvious dopesickness, a way to inquire into my well-being without seeming callous. Even with the heat on full blast and my clothes reeking of sweat, I could smell the peppermint on his breath. Over the sound of the AC, his breathing was still audible—heavy, but even.

"This is it," he announced, and tugged the key out of the ignition, throwing me a sideways smile.

Moroccan carpets, stained wood tables and stools, faux-leather couches and chairs, red lampshades, framed posters of old foreign films, the lingering aroma of incense and steamed vegetables. No liquor cabinets, as far as I could see.

Everything in earth tones, tastefully antiquarian. Only soft lighting, none from overhead.

"Tea?" Doc called back to me, walking into the kitchen.

"Sure," I said. I unwrapped my scarf and set it on top of my backpack by the door.

It was spacious inside, and not nearly as hot as it had been in the car. Doc had done well for himself—assuming, of course, that this was all his doing. Seeing how I'd never seen a ring on his finger, even years ago when I would visit him once a week, it was probably a safe enough guess.

He stood, back turned to me, at the sink, filling a teakettle with water.

"Take a seat," he said.

"How familiar," I retorted. "Old habits, Doc?"

He chuckled.

I took a seat and we sat in silence while the water got hot. I realized he was waiting for me to say something, but I didn't know the best thing to say, what he wanted me to say. When the teakettle screeched, he got up and turned off the burner, poured two cups.

"Green or Sleepy Time?" he asked.

"Green," I said. I wanted something sharp, astringent.

There was an unmistakable motherly quality about him, a quality that may have had its roots in a good upbringing or, more likely, in earnest, spiteful cultivation. Looking around the kitchen,

40

I realized that almost every detail in the house spoke of lonesomeness; each item in its place, untouched by outside forces or childish anarchy. Maybe *hermitage*, rather than lonesomeness, was the better word. It was hard to think of Doc as a victim.

He handed me my cup. As he leaned forward into the warm suffusion of light coming in from the living room, I noted his recently plucked eyebrows, the skin around them flushed and pink, the eyebrows themselves sharp apostrophes.

"So, Daniel," he said. "Why the call?"

"I finished my sixty days in-patient."

"Congratulations."

"Thought you might be proud."

"I *am* proud," he said. "Very proud. You've come a long way." He had this endearing and inexplicable way—where other people would just make you roll your eyes—of getting the most out of clichés. "But," he said, "that doesn't quite answer my question."

"And," I said, "my mom died."

"Oh." He grimaced, flashing two rows of perfectly straight, unstained teeth. "I'm so sorry, Daniel," he said. "When?"

I brought the cup to my lips, but the water was still too hot. I set it back on the table. I wondered if he'd smelled the cigarettes on me when I got into the car, and if it had made him feel like a failure. "A few months ago," I said. "Before I went in."

His brows scrunched into commas.

"Overdose," I went on, knowing he wanted me to. Even though it scalded my tongue, I forced myself to take a sip of tea. "I OD'd like a week after she did, at the reception."

"At the funeral reception?"

"In the bathroom."

"Jesus. Was your sister there?"

"I don't know, I was loaded."

"You don't know where your sister was?"

"She probably showed up. You know how she is."

He looked at me.

"She's better off without us, Doc."

"Daniel. Don't say shit like that."

In spite of everything, I almost smiled. This was why I'd always liked him.

From the kitchen we could see into the living room, the light from the setting sun spilling in deeper through the window, illuminating a vintage dollhouse that I hadn't noticed sitting on the coffee table. It was like one you'd see in an old Barbie commercial, sliced in half and two-storied, furnished precisely, almost a mirror image of the house encasing it.

"She was there," I said. "I remember her being there, I think. But we didn't talk. Still haven't."

The tea, or maybe just the warmth of the house, was finally starting to thaw me. Almost eight weeks clean, but still my body acted like an old engine in winter.

Doc pivoted. "No matter what your mind may tell you, Daniel," he said, "you took accountability. Positive action. I admire that."

I nodded, having a hard time looking him in the eye.

"Don't forget that."

"Can I use your restroom?" I asked.

He pointed me down the hall.

Doc been a good counsellor, one of the better ones I'd had—probably the best, for whatever that's worth. He'd always try to work some pseudo-Eastern philosophy stuff into our sessions, try to give the old model an interesting spin that he hoped would get through to me. "Live in the moment," was one of his lines. But what's the difference between that and living moment-*to*-moment? I'd always wondered, and never figured out, never bothering to ask him.

The hall was mostly in shadow. I walked past a row of watercolors lit by an old lamp, trying to shake my clothes dry of sweat. I closed the bathroom door behind me, turned on the light, opened the medicine cabinet. No pill bottles, no medications. But a jar. And inside the jar, a blue man.

He was a very small man, naked, maybe six inches tall. At first, because of the long hair, I thought he was a woman. With wide, imploring eyes he gazed up at me, as if he'd been waiting for me. Holes had been made in the cork lid. His hands pressed against the glass. He mouthed words, some of which I could probably hazard but chose not to. Some of his hair was missing, patchy strands of it confused across his bony shoulders. I eyed the tweezers sitting next to the jar. He followed my gaze, looked back at me, mouth open, expectant.

I shut the medicine cabinet. I pissed in the toilet, washed my hands afterwards, drying them slowly with hand towels. The towels had been pristinely folded and fluffed, but were lank and sodden when I put them back. I turned off the light and walked down the hall, head down, toward the row of watercolors lit by the old lamp. Standing at the end of the hall was Doc. I stopped.

"I made a bed for you," he said. "Next to the couch are some extra pillows and blankets, if you need them. You can stay here, of course, but I understand if you'd rather not."

"Thanks," I said, wondering if he could see the yearning in my eyes. Had he ever?

I approached him. He seemed—uncharacteristically—to be unsure of what to say next. When he didn't move, I stepped closer.

"You never did answer my question," he said finally.

"You're the last house on the block, Doc." I smiled weakly.

"There's a lot of time left, Daniel," he said. "You're on the right path."

With my next step, I was standing in the glow of the old lamp and feeling like someone had set fire to me. "Can you just hold me?" I heard myself saying. "Can we just lie down and you… hold me?"

"Daniel." His shoulders sagged, he looked down. "That's not a good idea," he said.

Not much space separated us now. I put my arms around him, sank my face into his chest. He resisted until he heard me choke back a sob. "Please," I said.

His bedroom was more modest than the rest of the house. A bed, a bedside table, blank walls save for one which was taken up by a bookshelf of old pulp sci-fi paperbacks and collectible action figures. On the edge of his bed, he cradled me in the spoon of his body, tense, breathing shallowly.

"I found the thing in the bathroom," I murmured, drinking in the smell of his forearm.

"What thing?" he said. There was no defensiveness in his voice.

I imagined him fucking me, not knowing what he's doing because he's never done a thing like this before, his dick long and thin and bursting through my asshole like a cattle prod, branding me on the inside. Choking gasps from above me, behind me, in the darkness of the room, him being very quick because he needs to be quick—to run from his better judgment, to put distance between the cathartic release of the present and the impending regret and self-loathing of tomorrow. *Live in the moment.* And when he comes inside me, the weight of five years' silence, repressed desire, second-guessing, and inner turmoil collapsing across my back in a sheen of sweat.

"Okay," I said. "I'll go to the couch now."

I got up, feeling Doc's body relax in the removal of mine. Stepping out of his bedroom, I went down the hall.

The little blue man jumped when I opened the medicine cabinet. He began beating at the walls of the jar, shrieking. Softly hushing him, I grabbed the jar, and was careful to pluck him out very gently.

His voice was so feeble and so small that I wouldn't have been able to make out his words if I wanted to. I held him in the palm of my left hand, stroked the mess of his hair with the fingers of my right hand.

How many times in rooms like this had I come across something not meant for my eyes? Bathrooms were not merely private places. A bathroom is a place of deep vulnerability. A raw place, a visible place.

She'd been in the tub a while, strung out, the water tepid. I'd just come home from school. But instead of rocking back and forth on the toilet seat with a spread of dirty gear at her feet and murmuring to me, over and over, the usual reasons why the fridge was empty, why my bike was gone, why my video games were gone, why my room had been turned upside down, my mom was oddly quiet. She spread her legs wide, her body warping beneath the sloshing waters, and said:

"Bury me in the clothes you find me in."

It came out as a croak, as if being in the water so long had turned her into an amphibian. Maybe it was this effect that made me do something I didn't normally do, which was ask why.

"People don't change, Danny."

I never uttered it, but the question still burned inside me: Bury you in the clothes you're in when I find you, Mom, or bury you in the clothes I'm wearing when I find you?

In the back of an ambulance, approximately twelve years after her offhanded and undoubtedly forgotten death pledge, and just under a month before I was admitted into rehab, my mother expired. We hadn't talked in a while. I don't know what she'd been wearing. I don't know if she'd changed, though the evidence pointed strongly to no. I didn't fault her for that.

I never faulted my sister, either, for writing us off. She was different from my mom and me— smarter, less moment-to-moment, and maybe that's what Doc had been trying to get at. When exactly my mom drew her last breath, I don't know; when exactly my sister and I last spoke, I don't know. I already knew more than I was supposed to.

There was a tingling in the middle of my palm, the little blue man squirming there, beating his fists into it. Not angrily, but in a rapturous outpouring of relief. He looked up at me, his face shiny with tears, like a little Christmas light. This time, I could hear what he said, the squeaks filling the void of the house. "Thank you," he said.

"I'm sorry," I said. I imagined my voice sounded colossal to him. Looking hard through my tears into his little eyes, I said, "It's just better this way," and I extended my arm to widen the gap between us. He looked at me quizzically, his face scrunching beneath his own sheen of tears.

"For everybody," I said, and took his head between my thumb and forefinger and popped it. His skull burst, and he fell limp, blood filling the creases of my palm. It was as red as mine.

I threw him into the toilet, washed the gore from my hands, soiling again the immaculate hand towels. I left the light on behind me, the toilet unflushed.

Doc was asleep now. I waited a while for my eyes to adjust to the darkness of the bedroom, an empty silence like a fist of air caught in my throat, and then I located his pants. I rifled through his wallet and plucked from it a handful of bills. From his shelf I grabbed an action figure, the box unopened. I wavered over to him through the ghostly morning solstice. The shape of his body beneath the covers was spliced into lines of gray from the shadows of the blinds. I caressed his wrist. I imagined him tomorrow looking at his wall and seeing the blank spot where his toy had been and wondering if there'd ever been anything there to begin with. Maybe he'd forget tonight. Maybe he'd forget his age. Maybe he'd start calling himself *Doc*, not knowing why. Maybe, hopefully, he'd forget me, and feel his own kind of dopesickness, one I never wanted to feel. One kind was enough.

I left the blinds as they were, the door unshut.

As I slunk down the hall, the fist of air dropped from my throat into my chest. I grabbed my backpack, exited through the front door, inhaled the sleepless day. The mantra reentered my brain, unsolicited.

(*Breathe. Breathe in the moment, breathe out the moment. Be. Breathe. Be. Don't confront it, don't run from it. Be it. Breathe. Be. Breathe. Live in the moment. Be it.*)

The sun fought through the clouds, but the neighborhood below remained gray, halved in cancerous light. I walked a few miles till I hit downtown, found a pawnshop, sold the action figure. Afterwards, I hailed a cab. I told the cabbie to take me to the bus station.

Which one?

The one a town over.

I flashed a few bills at him, and he nodded. On the drive, I contemplated my next move.

Kicks were getting harder to come by.

9 781908 125651